Mr. Katz and Me

By Marc Kornblatt
Illustrated by Nanette Regan

APPLES & HONEY PRESS

To Judith, my student, my teacher,
my wife, and my dearest friend.
— M. K.

Apples & Honey Press
An Imprint of Behrman House Publishers
Millburn, New Jersey 07041
www.applesandhoneypress.com

ISBN 978-1-68115-644-6

Library of Congress Cataloging-in-Publication Data

Names: Kornblatt, Marc, author. | Regan, Nanette, illustrator.
Title: Mr. Katz and me / by Marc Kornblatt ; illustrated by Nanette Regan.
Description: Millburn, New Jersey : Apples & Honey Press, 2024. | Audience: Ages 6-8.
| Audience: Grades 2-3. | Summary: A young girl befriends one of her father's
B'nai Mitzvah students, an elderly Russian immigrant named Mr. Katz.
Identifiers: LCCN 2023050969 | ISBN 9781681156446 (hardcover)
Subjects: CYAC: Jews—United States—Fiction. | Friendship—Fiction. |
Bar mitzvah—Fiction. | LCGFT: Picture books.
Classification: LCC PZ7.K8373 Mr 2024 | DDC [E]—dc23
LC record available at https://lccn.loc.gov/2023050969

Design by Elynn Cohen
Edited by Deborah Bodin Cohen
Printed in China

1 3 5 7 9 8 6 4 2

0125/B2759/A6

SOME NIGHTS, after dinner, kids come to our house to learn how to sing with my father. If they agree, my father lets me sit in the den to listen.

Some sing high.

Some sing low.

Some sing like canaries,

others like crows.

One evening, a tall, wrinkled man with an accent came to our house for bar mitzvah lessons too.

"How can you have a bar mitzvah?" I asked. "You're way past thirteen."

"Sarah." My father frowned, and I felt embarrassed for being rude. After all, the man was trying to learn something new.

The old man smiled.
"Such is life, *maideleh.*"

"What's a *maideleh*?"

"It's what we call a little girl in Yiddish."

"I'm not so little. I'm in second grade."

"You're right." He held out his hand. "Saul Katz. A pleasure."

His fingers trembled in mine. Most of my father's students are nervous at the beginning.

I thought Mr. Katz might be nervous too.
But he said he would be honored if I
listened, and so I could tell that he wasn't.

He was very polite. When he read a B sound instead of a V sound and my father corrected him, Mr. Katz said, "Thank you."

Every time my father corrected him,
he said the same thing, "Thank you."

Mr. Katz saw me staring at him and winked like we shared a secret.

I hardly knew him, so I didn't wink back.

At break time, I helped my mother serve a snack.

As I handed him his cup, Mr. Katz dropped it. Hot tea splashed on my feet.

"Oh no," I cried angrily. "My new shoes!"

"Forgive me," said Mr. Katz. "My hands have grown clumsy."

"You drop things too," my mother told me. I realized she was right and that I should be more patient.

The next time Mr. Katz came to our house, I was at the front window teaching myself how to draw a blue jay.

"Will you sit with us again?" he asked.
"I'm pretty busy," I told him, which wasn't really true.

"I understand." He winked. "I love birds."

"You're a Katz who loves birds?" I asked.

"Exactly," he said. And we both smiled.

When he opened his briefcase, it was empty.

"Did you forget your book?" I asked.

"Yes," Mr. Katz replied. "But I did remember to come."

That made me laugh. He laughed too.

It felt good to laugh together.

And I decided that I wasn't too busy to sit with him after all.

Dad loaned Mr. Katz a Hebrew reader. It was the same one I had.

"How old are you?" I asked.

"I am eighty-one years young," Mr. Katz replied.

"I'm eight," I said. "And we have the same reading book?"

He nodded. "A wonderful coincidence, ey *maideleh*?"

Mr. Katz's memory was as shaky as his hands, but he was a good student. After a few weeks, he could read better than me. It made me want to study harder.

When he chanted, his voice sounded as sweet as a canary, only deeper.

I sounded like a duck.

I wished I could sing like him.

One night, I asked Mr. Katz why he never had a bar mitzvah.

"Because in Russia, where I was born, having a bar mitzvah was dangerous," he said.

"Such things were forbidden. The government closed our synagogues and our Hebrew schools.

They made fun of our names and how we looked. We had to hide who we were."

"Were you afraid?" I asked.

"Sometimes," he said quietly.

"I would have been scared all the time," I said.

"Mostly I was angry," he said.

"So that's why you came here?" I asked gently.

"Yes. To be free. It wasn't fair of them to treat us like we didn't belong," he explained.

"When I first arrived in this country, I thought it was too late to have a bar mitzvah. Then I met your *tatelah*."

"My father?"

"Yes."

I smiled at him. "I'm glad you met him."

Mr. Katz smiled back.

"I am glad that you are glad, Sarahleh."

The night of his last lesson, I hummed along quietly.

After he was done, Mr. Katz hugged my father. He kissed
my hand, and we hugged too.

At his bar mitzvah, when his voice echoed across our synagogue sanctuary, it gave me goosebumps. I was proud to be his friend.

Even though he has already had his bar mitzvah,
Mr. Katz keeps coming to our house once a week
for tea and cookies.

But he doesn't sing with my father.

He sings with me.

When I chant at my bat mitzvah,
I want to sound like a canary too.

Author's Note

Sarah and Mr. Katz become friends despite the difference in their ages and backgrounds. A shared interest in singing and a similar sense of humor connect them. While Sarah learns empathy and patience through their friendship, Mr. Katz successfully closes a cultural gap so common for new immigrants. Think about your friends. What special qualities do they have? What does it mean to you to be a good friend?

This story was inspired by my family history. My grandfather Samuel Katznelson immigrated to the United States from the part of the Russian Empire now called Belarus, around 1905. He fled his country because of attacks, known as pogroms, on Jews. He wanted to live in a land where he could practice his religion without fear. In America, Papa Sam was a bar mitzvah tutor. I too became a tutor when I got older. My children became friends with one particular student of mine, an elderly man named Sol Kleiman. Have you ever been friends with somebody from a different generation? What did you learn from that friendship?

Like Mr. Katz in this story, Sol immigrated to America in the 1980s. He was part of a movement made up of Jews who emigrated from the Soviet Union because the government suppressed their religious practice by closing synagogues and Jewish cultural centers.

I hope this story inspires you to seek out new friends who have a variety of backgrounds and life experiences. May those friendships enrich your life.

Marc